A New School for Emily

Written by Marianne Posadas
Illustrated by Susy Boyer

Contents

NELSON
CENGAGE Learning
For learning solutions, visit **cengage.com.au**

Meet the Characters

Emily

The new girl at school.

Morgan

Emily's first friend.

Mr Vincenti

The teacher.

Holly

One of Emily's classmates.

Maisy

Another of Emily's classmates.

Dear Reader

Starting at a new school can be hard – I know, because I went to six different schools when I was a kid. I had to make new friends at each one. This story is about a girl who starts out by choosing the wrong friends ... I hope you enjoy it!

Marianne Posadas
Author

Emily's New School

1. Playground
2. Principal's office
3. Emily's classroom
4. Basketball court

1 A New School

Hi, my name's Emily. Have you ever had to move to a new school? A brand new school where you don't know anybody or anything? I have. It's not easy.

Dear Diary: Today I'm starting at another new school. I feel sick in my stomach. I want to stay home, but I can't. I wish I were at my old school, where all my friends are. I wish we hadn't moved to a new town. I want to tell Mum how I really feel, but I can't.

I'm nine years old and already I've been to six schools in three states. That's got to be a record, I'm sure of it.

My mum and dad have really excellent jobs – excellent for them, but not for me. They sell toys – very COOL toys.

I know – you must be thinking that would be so fantastic, having parents who sell toys. But it's not.

You see, they're opening lots of toy stores, all over the country. That's why we keep moving.

Mum and Dad spend six months doing all the work that's needed for opening up a store and then we move to the next city. When will it stop?

Dad says we'll stop when I'm in Year 7. That's six more stores, six more schools and three more years! I feel sick!

Suddenly my mobile phone beeps. It's a text message.

I open it and it's Delta, my best friend from my old school.

"WHATS HAPPNG? WHATS THE NU SCHOOL LIKE? GOT NU FRIENDS? MISS U! D."

I text back:

"MISS U 2. BOUT 2 LEAVE NOW. WILL TXT L8R."

I press "send", with a sad heart.

Mum's in the car, tooting.

I quickly put my diary in my bag and head for the door. It's time!

2 On My Own

Dear Diary: It's now lunchtime and I've been here for three hours, 45 minutes and 30 seconds! It feels more like three years, 45 days and 30 hours!

Mr Vincenti, my new teacher, seems nice. But I wish I were at my familiar old desk, at my familiar old school. Right now, I feel invisible, like a gigantic hollow bubble.

I'm eating my lunch … on my own. That's normal for all my first days at new schools. I bite into the bread roll that Mum made for me.

A whole dollop of hummus squirts out the sides and onto my uniform! Great! Humiliation already. I sneak a look around but no one's seen what happened.

Some of the kids from my class are playing basketball, making up rhymes to the beat of the bouncing ball.

That's one thing I know I'm talented at. I like rhymes and the way words sound when you combine them with a tune. Maybe I'll write a hit song or an advertising jingle one day. Then I'll be a famous composer, and everyone will know me when I go to a new school.

Bounce the ball, slower, faster
My bouncing's better than yours!
Mister, master, slower, faster
Watch me beat your scores!
Mister, master, slower, faster …
"Trip me if you dare!
Mister, master, slower, faster,
Slam-dunk through the air!"

I smile. The girls stop bouncing the basketball and stare at me like I'm an alien from outer space. One of the girls, Holly, smiles back though.

"Hey, that's pretty cool, Emily," she says.

I'm glad she remembers my name. "Did they sing that at your last school?"

"I just invented it," I say. Holly smiles again, and the girls go back to bouncing the basketball. She seems nice.

I feel better already.

3 A New Friend

I really miss my friends. But at least someone talked to me, and even remembered my name. That made me feel a whole lot happier. I guess that means I'm not really invisible. Maybe this school is going to be OK after all.

After lunch, things improve even more. For our writing lesson, Mr Vincenti says we're going to be composing poems. Cool. We have to write a three-line poem about something we feel. It's got to have emotion. I finish early.

I feel sad no one knows my name.
They all think I'm different,
But I'm just the same.

The girl sitting next to me leans over. She's got tightly curled red hair, and I've seen her with lots of friends.

"What did you write?" she asks. "I can't think of anything."

"What's your name?" I say. "What are you feeling right now?"

"Morgan," she replies. "And I'm feeling extra cool, thanks."

So I wrote a poem for Morgan.

I'm extra cool, the way I like to be!
If you need to chill out, too,
then hang around with me!

Morgan grins.

"You got that right," she says. "Thanks."

It's nice when someone else likes your rhymes, too. Especially a girl who seems to be pretty popular, like Morgan.

"Hey, do you want to see a really excellent trick?" she whispers. She pulls her mobile phone out of her pencil case and flips it open under the desk where no one can see what she's doing.

"What are you up to?" I ask anxiously. I know the rules. "We can't turn those on until after school!"

Morgan wrinkles her nose like she doesn't really care, and quickly keys in a text message.

"Now I send it to everyone in the class," she whispers. "Anyone who forgot to turn off their phone will get into trouble!"

Sure enough, as soon as she presses "send", someone's phone beeps loudly. I have to agree, it's a good trick!

The whole class turns around to see who it is.

It was Holly, the girl from basketball. Morgan and her friends snigger and point at her. Mr Vincenti frowns. He looks surprised.

"Sorry, Holly!" he says. "But you know the rules of our classroom. Hand over your phone. You can have it back at the end of the day."

4 Funny Rhymes

Dear Diary: It's been two days at my new school now. Things feel a bit better. I'm sorry about the tricks we play on Holly, because she seems quite nice. But Morgan and her friends are cool to hang around with, and they laugh at my poems and jokes. And they like my rhymes. Maybe they will be my new friends? I hope so.

At breakfast, I send a text to my old friend, Delta.

"HI D. HOPE U R OK. IM GOOD. HOWS MR SIMONS B.O.???"

I giggled. Mr Simon taught mathematics at my old school.

My phone beeped.

"EEW! JST THE SAME. U SOUND BETTA!"

Mum toots the horn. It's time to leave for school. I'm looking forward to seeing Morgan again.

During break, we make up hilarious songs about other children in the class. Morgan and her friends think my poems are so cool.

And then, just before lunch, Morgan points out Maisy. Maisy's so quiet, I haven't even noticed her much. I know she's one of the kids in the basketball team, but I've never heard her say anything.

"Let's get Maisy," says Morgan. "She smells. Write a poem about her."

I don't think Maisy smells. She seems OK.

But Morgan and her friends gather round and start giggling.

I'd better write something. I don't want to disappoint them.

I scribble on a piece of paper until some words start to rhyme.

Maisy is so quiet
That never could you tell
That Maisy has two stinky feet
That give off such a smell!

Morgan laughed. "Do another one, Emily," she said.

Maisy is a girl
Who smells like rotten eggs
She's got dirty rotten armpits
And smelly, hairy legs.

I notice Holly and Maisy looking over at us, but Morgan and I just stare back. We don't need them. My friends and I are cool.

Just before the bell, Morgan checks her phone. "My battery's low," she says. "Can I borrow yours?"

"Sure," I say, handing my phone over. I wonder who'll get caught. The texting trick is funny.

Morgan keys in a text and presses "send". But everyone is being extra careful today. No one's phone beeps.

"It doesn't matter," says Morgan. "That'll be a wonderful surprise for them when they get it tonight."

5 Something Is Wrong

Dear Diary: My whole weekend was wasted unpacking boxes with Mum and Dad. Dad says he never knew how many possessions we had! It's ridiculous. Mum says she's looking forward to the day we never have to use cardboard boxes and newspapers, ever again. I AM, TOO!

Today is the start of my second week and I'm actually glad to hear Mum tooting the car horn. That's until I get to school. After assembly, we go to our classroom. Something's wrong.

Mr Vincenti leans against the edge of his desk, looking stern. Everyone is quiet.

"Class," he says. "It has been reported to me that someone has been bullying other students in our classroom."

I feel sorry for whoever it was that got bullied. I got nasty bruises at a school last year, and it made me feel anxious all the time.

Suddenly Mr Vincenti's voice interrupts my thoughts.

"I want everyone to turn on their mobile phones, please," says Mr Vincenti.

I look across at Morgan, who keeps looking at the floor. Why won't she look at me? Why does Mr Vincenti want us to turn our phones on? This is weird.

Then Mr Vincenti pulls a mobile phone out of his briefcase. He keys in "reply". He holds up the phone.

"I'm disappointed to say that someone in this class has been text bullying," he says. "Sending mean texts. And I'm going to find out who."

And then I notice Maisy isn't in class. I have a sinking feeling in my stomach. I feel sick. I stare over at Morgan, but she's looking straight ahead at the mobile

phone that Mr Vincenti's holding. Maisy's mobile phone.

The teacher presses "reply".

MY PHONE BEEPS.

Dear Diary: The rest of Monday was totally horrible. No one talked to me. Not even Morgan. Everyone in the classroom avoided me like I had some kind of disgusting disease. I feel really bad. I was just trying to make friends, but Morgan tricked me. She's not my friend at all.

And worst of all, I've been horrible to a girl that I don't even know.

I feel like I want to move to a new school again. I never thought I'd say that.

Mum's silent on the drive home. I don't know whether she's upset at me or really disappointed. Mr Vincenti asked her to come to school early, and explained what had happened. My mum couldn't believe what I'd done – and, to be honest, neither could I. I feel sick again.

We eat our dinner in silence and Mum makes me go to bed early.

Dad looks really disappointed.

I sit on the edge of my bed and look at the cardboard boxes around me.

I feel in my pocket for my phone. I don't even feel like texting Delta. I feel like throwing it out the window.

But I don't. Sitting here in the darkness of my bedroom, I suddenly know what I have to do.

6 Can We Be Friends?

You can pack a lot of stuff in cardboard boxes. But there are some things you can't.

Like friends.

Even if we only stay here for six months, I'm going to start acting like this is going to be my home.

Somewhere I'll be happy. And that means I have to make some decisions and change my behaviour.

I look up my "dialled numbers" page. I take a deep breath. I push "call back".

Someone answers. I know the voice.

"Maisy?" I say. "It's Emily. I'm sorry. What I did was wrong. I'm sorry it made you feel bad. It will not happen again. Can we be friends?"

She hesitates.

"I guess."

We talk. She's nice to me, and I feel better. I think she feels better, too.

When I go to school tomorrow, I've promised myself I'm making a fresh start. I'll be behaving the way I want to, not the way that Morgan and those girls expect me to. I don't feel sick anymore. I'm just looking forward to being with my friends.

My *new* friends.

THE END